I0584197

NIGHT OFFICE

ASSET RESOURCE MANAGEMENT

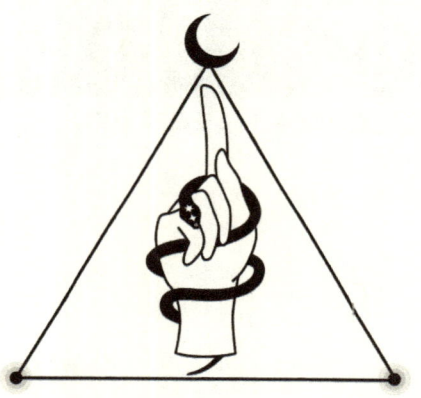

NIGHT OFFICE

THE DOOM THAT CAME TO THE COFFEE SHOP

COMPILED BY **MARK TEPPO**

ASSET RESOURCE MANAGEMENT

EAE–103/c   FOR INTERNAL USE ONLY

51325 Books

Produced in association with **51325 Books** and Firebird Creative, LLC (Clackamas, OR).

How hard can it be to order a cup of coffee?

A Night Office publication
ARM – EAE – 103/c
rev. 21/ ed. 05.2022

http://nightoffice.org

ASSET RESOURCE MANAGEMENT

THE DOOM THAT CAME TO THE COFFEE SHOP

EAE-103/c

SCOPE: This educational assessment exercise is offered by Night Office Asset Resource Management as an outreach opportunity for potential Asset Resource Management field operative candidates. The exercise attempts to provide an example of the mental acuity, psychological stability, and intellectual resourcefulness required to perform the extremely nuanced and occasionally irrational duties of a Night Office field operative.

Given the complex nth-dimensional sub-structures of the psychological matrices developed by the Night Office and of the unmanaged nature of these educational assessment exercises, no assessment score will be provided. Commentary in regards to the relative success or failure of any given end point within this exercise is provided to downplay any lasting mental, emotional, physical, or psychological scarring that may result as having participated in this educational assessment exercise.

Night Office Asset Resource Management makes every effort to present these educational assessment exercises in accordance with the most current policies, procedures, and practical applications of relevant esoteric knowledge, but Night Office Asset Resource Management offers no assurances that these materials are truly up-to-date.

AUDIENCE: The intended audience for this educational assessment exercise are individuals who have either performed poorly on other assessment exercises offered by the Night Office or who are interested in applying for a Night Office field operative position, but who lack familiarity with how the Night Office works.

A copy of a fully executed Standard Non-Disclosure Agreement (Form PALM—DLT—23/d) is required. Please ensure that your form is properly filed before beginning this educational assessment exercise.

DISCLAIMER: This educational assessment exercise is intended to familiarize potential field operative candidates with workplace hazards, mental health stressors, and other psychological complexities that may present themselves during the course of performing designated Night Office tasks. While Night Office Asset Resource Management has attempted to thoroughly address all possible scenarios and outcomes of these educational assessment exercises, it is entirely likely that new stressors, hazards, and other causes for psychotic breaks may present themselves as a result of, or during the process of, or in the aftermath of completing this exercise. To the extend that local, state, and federal guidelines, mandates, and statutes regarding extra-terrestrial entities, cosmic fungi, and other non-Euclidean monstrosities even exist, Night Office Asset Resource Management makes no guarantee that procedures, policies, and practices as suggested in this assessment exercise make any effort whatsoever to follow these existing guidelines, mandates, and statutes. Nor does Night Office Asset Resource Management assume any responsibility—implied, implicit, or suggested to the contrary—for psychological, physical, and/or mental damage, grief, or distress a potential candidate may incur as a result of, or during the process of, or in the aftermath of completing this educational assessment.

INSTRUCTIONS: This Night Office Asset Resource Management educational assessment exercise is a series of interwoven narrative choices that will test your mental acuity and psychological alacrity. At the end of each passage, the candidate will be provided with a variety of narrative options. It is up to the candidate to decide which path is the correct path. Candidates should continue to explore narrative branches until they reach an end point, where they will find a summary statement.

Certain solutions may provide a complimentary coffee voucher. Please do not use the coffee voucher prior to completing this educational assessment exercise. That would be rude, and it is not the sort of out of box thinking that Asset Resource Management talks about when it says it is interested in "creative solutions."

SHORT FORM ACKNOWLEDGMENT: The act of turning this page is a tacit acknowledgment on the part of the candidate that they are engaging in this educational assessment exercise, and that they do so of their own volition.

Candidates further acknowledge that they are not being forced to undertake this assessment as a proxy agent for another individual, being, or entity that might have co-opted their intelligence.

Read & Understood: _____
[initials]

1

This is a test. This is only a test. It will not hurt. Well, okay. It might hurt a little bit. But you're ready for that, aren't you? You are an adventurous reader—rather, you like to think you are, and that's fine. We don't mind.

Oh, yes? Us? Don't worry about that right now. Focus more on the test. That one that is about to begin.

Right now, in fact.

You see a door in front of you. It is marked "The Abyss."

Do you open the door?

Yes, you open the door.
Go to 2.

Oh. You have more questions?
Go to 3.

2

You open the door marked "The Abyss."

Beyond is an endless void, bound by infinity and surrounded by the Ineffable. There is nothing, and beneath that nothing is everything.

This void looks at you.

You stare back. You can't help yourself (plus what else is there to look at in here?). Guess what? This is exactly what you are not supposed to do. Why? Because to look upon the void and have it look at you will shred your soul into tiny little mewling bits.

For the record, this is one of many terminal points in this exercise, and they will be rendered like this:

CONGRATULATIONS. YOU ARE A PILE OF MEWLING BITS.

What did you think was going to happen? You opened a door labeled "Herein Lies Monsters," and sure enough, there were monsters. Well, *one* monster, but it's very large. Its sole purpose is to suck your soul out through your eyeballs when you gaze upon it, and that's pretty much what it did, so there you go.

For the record, this is a dumb way to die.

Now, you could give this test to a friend and tell them to open the door too. "Hey, see what happens. Come on. I did it!" And what do you know? That friend will be dead too.

You won't be the only idiot in the endless void, so you'll have that going for you.

Don't be disappointed with yourself. This is how the human animal learns. Now that you know what's at stake, you're going to take this exercise more seriously, aren't you?

Plus, we get better data out from this educational assessment exercise if you actually try, so it's a win for everyone!

Do you feel properly chastised for falling for the dumbest

trick in the book? And no, we don't care that you haven't read the "book" we're referencing here.

Go to 4.

This may feel like a cheap trick and you may feel a little frustrated with our tone, but you know what? That's just your opinion. We've been doing this for over a hundred years. We know a little something about surviving alien invasions.

Regardless, time to suck it up and start over. Try not to open the door this time.

Got to 1.

3

This is a test. It measures your mental stability.

In the olden times (read last century), people went mad when they found weird manuscripts filled with arcane secrets. You would think that successive generations would learn to:

a) not open books with covers made from human flesh; or

b) not intone cryptic incantations that fall under the category of "Summoning Vast Intelligences That See Humanity As a Stain on the Cosmos;" or

c) not wander into dark places because they thought they heard something and it'll only a take a minute and what harm could come from looking, right?

But no, successive generations still fall for that shit.

The Night Office believes we can protect the human brain from exposure to cosmic horror, clickbait pop-up spamming, and endless parades of cute animal gifs that seem adorable but are really tragic pleas for help disguised by some idiot's poorly constructed meme phrase that is, of course, set in Times New Roman. This only serves to increase the horror ten-fold.

In short, we are here to help. This test is meant to strength your tolerance to self-referential deconstructionism and glimpses of the cosmic void wherein all thought and identity are obliterated.

This test is not graded on a curve. It is merely pass or fail, though we pride ourselves on an exceptionally high pass rate when students have partaken of at least thirteen hours of specialized online coaching, which is available from your account executive.

Already completed your online coaching sessions?

Go to 7.

If you weren't aware that online coaching was necessary,

but suspect that it is mostly a scam meant to drain your bank account, you'd be right.

Go to 7 (but do so with full confidence of your insight).

Not sure about what is going on here?

[It's the exit. Never mind what's actually written on the door. Just open it. Go on. Yep, right now. Off you go!]

Go to 2.

4

Hello. This is a test. This is only a—oh, what? You've been here before. Okay. Okay. We don't need to go over this part again.

So, getting on to things . . .

You see a door in front of you. It is marked "The Abyss."

You suspect this is a trap. But you are still going to open that door, aren't you?

Go to 5.

No, you learned something from the last time you were given this choice.

Go to 3.

5

Seriously?

Well, guess what? The Abyss is still there, and it still looks at you first.

You can't sneak up on the Abyss. Really. A lot of people—smart people, in fact—have tried. They failed too. In fact, they're out there, floating about. They're not bumping into each other, because, you know, endless void and all.

Still, it is comforting to know you're not the only one who can't follow directions.

We should give you another try, shouldn't we? This is, after all, only a test, which, presumably, you can't fail.

Yet here we are, right?

Anyway, if you'd like another restart:
Go to 6.

If you find the tone of this educational assessment exercise not to your liking and would prefer something a little less taxing:
Go to 61.

6

Hello. This is a test. This is—oh, too busy to hear the instructions, are you? Fine. Fine. Let's just get to it.

Before you is a door marked "The Abyss." It has been nailed shut, so don't even think about it.
Go to 3.

7

This is a test. It is meant to chart mental acuity, psychic strength, and your ability to withstand deep states of disorientation and bureaucratic distress. The test may have begun already. The test will require you to imagine an extended scenario that may or may not have positive solutions, e.g. you may die often. Do not be alarmed. We are charting your ongoing emotional state in regards to a variety of psychological and neurological triggers associated with dismemberment, deceleration trauma, shark attacks, getting stabbed in an alley, suffocation, being burned alive, being attacked by voles, dehydration, exsanguination, strangulation, getting poked in the eye with a sharp stick, and having every molecule of your being disassociated from consensual reality.

Also, we can guarantee there will be tentacled horrors. Regardless of how you answer.

Plan accordingly.

Ready to start now?
Go to 9.

Maybe not quite yet.
Go to 8.

8

We would like to remind you that the complimentary coffee voucher (a $3 value) is only available upon completion of the test.

What? Three dollars isn't enough? That's something you should take up with your local coffee shop. We don't set pricing, and frankly, we're outraged by the naked capitalist greed on display with some of these prices. It's a cup of milk with an ounce of hot water steamed through a hard puck of over-roasted not-as-fair-trade-as-you-think coffee beans. Profit margin is what? six hundred percent?

So, it's not on us if you feel taken advantage of here. It's the system. It's designed to make you feel impotent and unimportant. It's designed to make you feel as if you don't matter, as if you are just a number attached to a constantly dwindling bank account. It will never be full enough, will it? Nothing will ever be enough for you. We could give you a $50 gift card, and you'd still bitch about how we left permanent creases on your frontal lobes with our instruments.

We didn't, by the way. Our technicians are more dextrous than that.

What? Like you noticed what they did back there.

Oh, sorry. Did we say the test was over?

Whoops.

Our bad.

Anyway, please continue.
Go to 9.

9

This test will immerse you in a psychological reconstruction of an imaginary expedition to an undisclosed site of Cyclopean architecture. The very sight of these towers will make you vomit and bleed from the eye sockets. You will be given a series of narrative choices that will take you on a dizzyingly complicated route through this city of batrachian eldritchosity.

We highly recommend not deviating from the route laid out for you. This route has been optimized to ensure the greatest chance of mental continuity. Go off the rails, and you will likely lose your mind.

You will not get the $3 complimentary coffee voucher if you go nuts. Keep that in mind if you feel an increasingly frantic urge to bail the fuck out. Don't do it. Finish the test.

It is the only way.

Trust us. We mean no harm.

We only want to help, but such assistance requires showing you the true nature of the universe, if only for a brief second.

That'll be enough. Trust us. We know.

Please turn to **SECTION 10** when you are ready to begin.

THIS PAGE WAS INTENTIONALLY LEFT BLANK . . .

BUT IT ISN'T, SO WHAT DOES THAT MEAN?

ARE THERE MICRODOTS READING YOUR INVOLUNATRY STRESS RESPONSES?

OR PERHAPS THERE'S SOMETHING IN THE PAPER THAT IS BEING ABSORBED BY YOUR SKIN.

MORE LIKELY, IT IS MERELY A LABOR-SAVING MEASURE THAT HAS A FINANCIAL BENEFIT OF NEARLY ZERO. HOWEVER, CONSIDERATION OF THIS PAGE MAY RAISE YOUR BASELINE LEVEL OF PSYCHOLOGICAL STRESS AND NEUROLOGICAL CONFUSION, WHICH WE ARE DEFINITELY CHARTING.

10

This educational assessment exercise is an immersive experience, optimized via next-generation subliminal rendering alpha-geometrics that will approximate reality in 84.7% of all subjects who engage with the exercise.

You may stop this exercise at any time. You may resume the exercise at any time. We do not guarantee the persistence of the experiential envelope during such time when you are not actively engaging with the exercise, though we are required by local, state, and federal statutes to note that this educational assessment exercise is highly experimental (though the delivery mechanism has been functionally the same for more than six hundred years), and that your retention of the material in the exercise, your emotional reactions to that same material, and any psychosomatic responses you may have to the material are probably not fully noted in our side-effect documentation.*

Please adhere to the previously stated guidelines of this educational assessment exercise, and we ask that you participate with fully mental awareness and presence at each decision point within the immersive narrative experience. Doing so will ensure both the quality of your experience, as well as the integrity of the collected data.

You may restart this educational assessment exercise at any point when you find yourself unable to continue the narrative. While persistent restarts of this exercise may result in a deeper immersion of the educational assessment narrative, such persistence may also increase the possibility of a psychotic break, thereby reducing your baseline morality index.

You acknowledge that you are a willful participant of this exercise, and that you undertake this exercise with full awareness of the parameters under which your mental acuity and resilience are being examined.

You acknowledge that the Night Office is not liable for any behavior modifications, neurological shifts, or psychological stressors that you may exhibit after completing this exercise.

If you find yourself unable to comply with these requirements, please discontinue this educational assessment exercise and dispose of it in an appropriate fashion.

It would be best if you didn't speak of your failure to be brave to anyone, because they will judge you.

Otherwise,
Go to 11.

*Available upon request. Receipt of such documentation may take 4 - 6 weeks. All Night Office documentation may change at any time without prior notice.

11

In the beginning, there is a coffee shop. It's a franchise coffee shop. You see them everywhere. They are ubiquitous and therefore, calming. Nothing could ever happen in such a place, because they are carefully constructed to be a thoroughly welcoming and non-confrontational place.

You enter this coffee shop. There is unobtrusive music playing. The furniture looks comfortable without being judgmental. The walls are painted in calming brown and gray tones. Attractive people who are in your age group and financial bracket are sitting at small tables, talking earnestly about important issues facing the world today.

Behind the counter, there are a dozen baristas whirling about in a complex choreography that ensures milk gets steamed, donuts get plated, and hot sandwiches get heated to an appropriate temperature.

There are five people in line with you.

This is the actual test, by the way. Those previous sections were meant to elicit a series of emotional and psychological responses. Some of it was meant to make you feel smart. Some of it probably made you feel not-so-smart. Some of it may have pissed you off. All of these emotional reactions are appropriate. The Night Office is interested in the range of emotional responses that you are capable of. No, we are not recording your emotional responses via pupil dilation, breath response, and stimulation of epidermal cells (regardless of what the blank page back there suggested). That sort of monitoring is wacky science fiction stuff, and we are not here to talk about sci-fi stuff. We're here to talk about monsters and your ability to face them.

We'd like you to survive these encounters. And yes, we understand that survival would be easier if you had cool science fiction type gear. Like elegant writing instruments that shot super lasers out of their tips. Or micro missiles that could be launched from a tiny slot in your cellphone. Or satellite-based ion cannons that could nuke this side of the planet from orbit (because that's the only way to be sure, right?)

Anyway, a great-great-great-great-great-great ancestor of yours once watched a Knight of the Realm disembowel a howling void sucker with a wooden spoon, so let's not pretend that the current level of technology isn't sufficient to save your ass, should the need arise.

Okay? Ready now?

You're in a coffee shop. Calming browns and grays. Baristas steaming milk, plating donuts, heating sandwiches. You know the setup. Don't dwell on it overmuch.

You and five other people are standing in line. A critical skill for Night Office field operatives is the ability to quickly assess the potential threat level of humanoids. Let's try it now.

Directly in front of you is an attractive fellow with dark hair and dark eyes. He is wearing leather shoes and he keeps looking at an expensive watch. He's got a copy of the local paper tucked under his arm. His suit jacket lays nicely across his broad back. It looks tailored.

Directly behind you is an older woman wearing Yoga pants and a fleece top. Her hair is held in place by a wide sweat band. She has a personal mug in one hand, and in her other hand is her phone. She is demonstrating the value of an opposable thumb in that she can hold the device and scroll its screen with one hand. There's a not-insignificant amount of peer-reviewed commentary that this physical skill isn't all that useful to the continued survival of the human species, but this is where we've gotten to in this century, so let's not be too down on our current evolutionary trajectory.

No, you can't tell what she's busy scrolling through. You're just going to have to wonder. It probably won't be relevant.

Behind her is a young man wearing a dark gray hoodie. His jeans are threatening to slide off his legs because he's wearing them in the current style that young men do, which is all about showing off their underwear. His boots are stained with mud. He's got a fidget, which you can't imagine more coffee is going to help.

The last person in this line is a professional woman dressed in a dark suit with a maroon blouse. Her hair is shellacked into a geometric shape, and her makeup is severe and mathematically precise. The line is clearly not moving fast enough for her schedule.

The reason the line isn't moving is the old man at the register. The barista has a patient look on her face, but you can tell her training does not include dealing with people who can't make up their fucking minds. The old man is staring at the flat panel displays behind the counter, which are rotating through an endless permutation of beverage options. The old man is frustrated because the menu pages are changing faster than he can read them. *You want a mocha? Too late. How about something made from tea? What kind of tea? Green tea? Red—oh, too late! It's time for pictures of sandwiches!*

A knot is forming between his eyebrows. His frustration is starting to turn into outrage.

What do you do?

Maybe you'll order a mocha.
Go to 12.

Perhaps a sandwich.
Go to 14.

12

The old man points at the menu screens. "There," he says quickly. "I'll have one of—"

The screens change as the barista looks over her shoulder. "A pot-roasted pork shoulder sandwich?" she asks.

"No, goddamn it," the old man snorts. "I wanted a latte."

"Those are donuts," the barista says, referencing what is on the screen now.

"I know what a fucking donut is," the old man snarls. "I didn't ask for one of those. I want a latte."

The barista blinks at him. Behind her, the screens change again. "What size?" she asks.

"I don't know," the old man says. His hands flutter, as if he's captured a hummingbird.

"A Supra? Okay." The barista nods, finally on familiar ground.

"No, wait. How big is that?" the old man asks.

Behind him, Watch Guy looks at his watch. Twelve and a half seconds have passed since he last looked.

"Seventy-two ounces," the barista says.

"Seventy-two?" The old man can't believe what he's hearing. He looks around at the line stacking up behind him. "Who needs that much coffee?"

"I do," Hoodie Guy pipes up.

The barista glances at him, a thin smile touching her lips. A spark passes between Hoodie Guy and the barista. They are simpatico in this regard. She'd like to slowly pour seventy-two ounces of hot coffee over his naked—

Oh, sorry. Did you think we were going to ask something about the people in line?

Go to 13.

Actually, you were distracted for a second there, thinking about a mocha flow of hot coffee. How it splashes off tight abdominal muscles. How it courses along canyons and ridges created by taut—

Go to 15.

13

This is the problem with having pre-existing expectations when you are on a field operation. If everything is normal, there's no reason for a Night Office field team. It's only when things are abnormal that the skills of Night Office field operatives are invaluable. Your ability to be flexible—to adjust on the fly—is one of the key metrics that determines your viability as a potential Night Office candidate.

Don't get hung up on what you think *might* be happening. Only focus on *what* is happening.

Now, where were we? Oh, yes, the old man getting irate about the relative serving size in this coffee shop. Hoodie Guy—well, we call him "Tweaker" in another thread, but that's a thread you didn't pick, so we should probably keep calling him "Hoodie Guy"—Hoodie Guy . . .

What? Are you wondering if this is the wrong thread? If we keep calling him "Hoodie Guy" that means this thread is never going to merge back with the other thread, which means there's an entirely different narrative you're never going to experience. Is that thread the one that gives a better score? Have you totally failed this experiment already?

Don't worry about it.

Oh, *not thinking* about that other thread is all you *can* think about now, thank you very much.

Go to 54.

Focus on this thread. The other thread is irrelevant because it isn't the thread you are in.

Go to 19.

14

The most critical question facing you is: What sandwich are you going to order?

Your choices are:

A pot-roasted pork shoulder sandwich with pickled onions.
Go to 22.

A free-ranged turkey and hand-cured cheddar sandwich, served on fresh-baked sourdough bread.
Go to 21.

Seriously? This is turning into a Pick A Sandwich Exercise?
Go to 23.

15

Incidentally, your hot and bothered creative visualization is interrupted by Hoodie Guy, who says something that sounds like "Buzz buzz frisky kumquat. Alpha. Dogma. I NEED SOME FUCKING COFFEE."

That last is pretty clear. In fact, everyone in the coffee shop is really aware of how strung out Hoodie Guy is.

In fact, let's upgrade him to Tweaker. That's a better name.

Anyway, Tweaker is losing his shit about how far away he is from getting his mainline of drip coffee (he's not into all that creamy nonsense they try to spoil his hot black tar with). He's weaving back and forth, one hand clutching at his pants to keep them from sliding off.

It's hard to think of how this guy could be a credible risk. If he lets go with that hand, his pants are heading for his ankles, which is going to restrict his movement. Since he isn't going to do that (we hope), you only have to keep track of his other hand. Simple enough, right?

Professional lady is trying to move him with her mind. You can see it in her eyes. After all the years of being not listened to in high school, all the years of being passed over for promotions by assholes whose only qualification for the job was that they were male, and all the years of men thinking an open barstool means an open invitation to sit down and leer, it's admirable that she thinks such mind powers actually exist.

Tweaker, however, is unaware of her penetrating gaze.

Exercise Grandma, on the other hand, is attuned to the female psyche. Even though she knows Professional Lady is not pissed at her, she can sense that Professional Lady is making with the "if my eyes were lasers, I'd be dicing you into very precise cubes" look.

Eventually, Exercise Grandma pulls her attention away from her phone. She looks up and notices Tweaker in line behind her.

"Oh. Dear," she says. She makes it two sentences.

"What's your problem, lady?" Tweaker snaps.

"You appear to have lost your belt," she says.

"Shut your mouth, you old bat," Tweaker says.

Tweaker tries to pull something from his hoodie. It catches on the fabric. He tilts to one side and loses his grip on his pants. They slide; he stumbles. The glass display case catches him, and he hangs there for a second, his pants sliding down at a rate that makes the next half-second seem like an eternity.

There's something in his hand.

"Gun!" you shout.
Go to 17.

"Dildo!" you shout.
Go to 20.

16

Look, there are all sorts of impossible situations to which there are no viable solutions. People die all the time because they can't figure out a way out of whatever terminal atrocity they've fallen into. On the one hand, this is Nature's way of culling the herd; on the other, it's Nature's way of saying "Grow some new neural pathways, you smooth-brained mouth-breathers."

Okay, Mother Nature is actually kinder than that, because she loves all of her miscreants equally, but you get the point. And yes, it does beg the question of what is the Night Office trying to prove here by putting you in an impossible situation, especially when we only give you two choices: "Ridiculous" and "Are You Fucking Kidding Me?" Trust us when we tell you we've got the statistical data to back up the factoid that both of those reactions crop up in 96.65% of field operations. Get used to having your mind blown, dear supplicant. It's the only way to survive.

In fact, here's another statistic: 100% of field operatives who survive a Night Office mission cite "being grounded" as a key facet of their success. Reality is going to get slippery when you start wrestling with trans-dimensional six-eyed cats from Oxqu. Maintaining a firm grip on reality is critical. You can't Open if you aren't grounded, and you certainly can't Close. We're not even going to talk about the Way. Not now. Not when you're filled with some much doubt.

Anyway, as much as it might seem otherwise, there are rules. You will follow them. Failure means death. It's as simple as that.

What are the rules?

We can't tell you.

The lack of transparency about the rules is bullshit.
Go to 32.

This sounds a lot like that temp job you had over the summer. You put up with the boss's nonsense for about six weeks. Then you swiped a whole bunch of office supplies, pissed in a jar you left in the staff refrigerator, and ordered a bunch of sex toys using a credit card you found in his desk drawer.

Anyway, you get it, don't you? There are no rules except the rules you make up—the ones that keep you alive. You can dig that.

Go to 33.

17

People scream. Someone throws a cup of coffee, and there's a beautiful freeze-frame moment when a spray of hot coffee is making an arc over someone's head as they stand in shock—their eyes bugging out of their heads, their mouths stretched wide. But everything speeds back up, and your cinema verité moment passes.

Tweaker puts his back against the display cabinet, and he's waving the object around. More people scream. Exercise Grandma has collapsed on the floor in front of you; she's either had a heart attack or she's playing dead. You can check in a moment.

You put your hands up, but then you realize what Tweaker is waving about isn't a gun. It's . . . another hand.

This one is all gnarly and mummified, and not at all like a pink and fleshy human hand. It looks like it has been burned, freeze-dried, and then burned again. It's the hand from a dead criminal, isn't it? And those are only good for one thing.

Oh, you don't know what the sanctified hand of a dead criminal is used for? Perhaps you should bone up on your occult reliquaries before you go any farther.
Go to 26.

Ah, this mean trouble.
Go to 28.

Wait. What about Exercise Grandma?
Go to 41.

18

The voucher looks like it has been printed on an office computer. The paper is cheap. It's one-sided. It's not even squarely cut. Wait, is this voucher even legit? Have we lured you into participating in a marketing exercise under false pretenses?

This wouldn't be the first time you've been lied to by a corporate entity, is it? There was that other time when you thought you were going to get all that free cat food and then—

Oh, look! The old dude has finally managed to convey his order to the barista. She's smiling and nodding at him. She tells him how much his beverage is going to be, and he's fumbling for his wallet. Oh, dear. Is he missing his wallet too?

Step up offer your voucher to the old man.
Go to 27.

You're starting to lose interest in this exercise.
Go to 55.

19

Well done. Staying focused is another critical Night Office field operative skill. Focus on the where, the who, and the how.

Where: coffee shop. Brown and gray. Steaming mugs. Hot donuts. Agitated people waiting for their caffeine fix.

Who: Old geezer who doesn't have the bladder capacity for seventy-two ounces. Attractive barista who is already bored with her shift and is quietly dying for something interesting to happen. Greasy-eyed wastrel with pants gravity is going to grab any second now.

How: How are you going to pay for whatever you order?

Ah, another curve ball. You didn't flinch with this one. You're getting the hang of it.

Okay, so this is a valid question: how are you going to pay for your order. Did you bring your wallet? You check your coat pockets. Nothing there. How about your pant pockets? Nothing there either—oh, wait. The coffee voucher?

No, you don't have that. You're not finished, so the voucher—

Oh, you want to use the voucher now?

Sure. Otherwise, this test is going to grind to a halt over an argument whether you even have the mental tools to complete the test. You know that's a trap. Why would anyone create a psychological evaluation tool that can't be solved? Sure, it was clever as a plot point in that science fiction movie you saw when you were younger and more impressionable, but come on, that sort of science fiction psychobabel isn't going to fly at the Night Office.

Go to 16.

However, if you take the voucher now, you will not be given a second one upon completion of this test. No, we are not trying to "weasel" out of our previous agreement. We're merely trying to play along as you decide to rewrite reality in the service of this narrative.

Oh, but this isn't real. Whereas the voucher offer for completion is. Are you sure about that? Have you see that voucher?

Yeah, we thought so.

Just take the damn voucher already.

Go to 18.

20

The scene freezes. Almost everyone was prepping for "gun!" but that's not what you said. You said something else entirely, and it is taking everyone a few seconds to process the mental image that you've thrust at them. Ah, metaphorically speaking, of course.

Though, judging by the tiny smirk on Professional Lady's face, she's had no trouble keeping up with you.

But you were right. He didn't have a gun. He has something else entirely. Something that isn't a sex toy. It's actually . . . another hand.

This one is all gnarly and mummified, and not at all like a pink and fleshy human hand. It looks like it has been burned, freeze-dried, and then burned again. It's still a hand from a dead body, though, and we know what those are good for, don't we?

Ah, no, actually. You have no idea what a hand from a dead man is for.

Go to 26.

Ah, this mean trouble.

Go to 28.

21

The free-range turkey and hand-cured cheddar, served on fresh-baked sourdough bread, is a fine sandwich. The crew member suggests a fizzy water to go with that sandwich, and you agree. That sounds like a fine idea. The crew member compliments you on your decision. "Excellent choice," they say.

You detect a small tremor in the crew member's voice when they say those words. *Excellent choice.*

You wonder if you're missing something here.
Go to 44.

This tremor might be the only clue you're going to get. Maybe you should look behind you.
Go to 46.

22

Ignoring the old dude who can't function well in modern society, as well as the Type A car salesman with massive insecurity issues, you move to the counter and inform the crew member that you'd like the pot-roasted pork shoulder and pickled onions sandwich.

"Good choice," the crew member says. "What would you like to drink with that?"

"Just the sandwich," you say.
Go to 42.

Crap. Now you have to figure out what to drink. And here you thought you were circumventing that whole track.
Go to 43.

23

The Night Office does not have to explain itself. It does not report to any agency other than itself. (And it's only measure of success is whether or not the human race is still here tomorrow, so let's keep that in mind, shall we?). The Night Office is amused by your efforts to second-guess its operating procedures, but only in the same way that a new pet owner is amused by a puppy's attempt to not trip over its own feet when it runs.

You don't have to take this test. You don't have to answer any of these questions. You can go back to a life of complete denial. You can keep pretending that the universe isn't filled with glorpy monstrosities that will devour your souls without a thought.

No, seriously. They don't have brains. They just eat the raw stuff that floats out there, waiting to be formed. This includes approximately eighty percent of what constitutes the human soul. The rest is, well, don't worry about that part. It's . . . complicated.

Anyway, the point here is that no one is forcing you to consider the great and meaningless void beyond the shelter of our tiny little marble hurtling through space. No one is saying, "Hey, none of it means anything, so do you think your fucking opinion matteres in the slightest?"

Statistically speaking, you will amount to nothing and no one will miss you, but that doesn't invalid your capacity for self-deception. You can lie to yourself. You have a boundless capacity for hope. For something different. For some sort of revelation. And that capacity is what sustains the human experiment.

So, yes, this may seem like nothing more than a dumb exercise where you have to choose between two sandwiches—even when you may not be hungry—but that is what this is all about. That is what the Night Office is all about.

It's not over if you can still make a choice. A choice implies hope. And hope is all we have.

So pick a damn sandwich already.

Fine. Turkey and cheddar on sourdough.
Go to 21.

Why does it have to be a sandwich? What if you want soup?
Go to 25.

24

"Look," you say to the barista. "We can stand here all day, waiting for this gentleman to remember where he left his wallet—"

"I left it in Jersey," the old man interrupts.

"—we can wait for him to go to New Jersey and get it," you amend. "Or, you can comp his beverage and move this line along."

The barista chews on their lower lip. This sort of decision is above their pay grade.

You make eye contact with the shift manager who has been standing there this whole time. Doing nothing, as far as you can tell, except stress all the crew members out. "You," you say, pointing at the shift manager. "How about you make a management decision here."

The shift manager's eyebrows go up. They look around, as if they can't believe you spotted them.

"This line isn't moving," you point out. "Your CPH is going to shit. You okay with that?"

While you have no insight into whether this coffee company calls their hourly metric "CPH"—"customers per hour"—you're confident the shift manager knows what you mean. The point is: *cash don't flow when the line don't roll*, as they used to say back when you worked in the retail services industry.

Crew members around the shift manager stop moving. Somewhere a lonely blender finishes its time-measured task and winds to a halt. It's quiet in the coffee shop. Even the canned music, which was recently playing a cover version of some classic soft rock song, is holding its breath.

You hear a brush of fabric against fabric behind you, and you know Executive Chucklehead has just checked his watch again.

"You're making him late," you say, indicating the man behind you with your thumb.

Farther down the line, the guy in the grey hoodie starts mumbling. Something about the heat death of the universe and faces melting—it's probably not important. Behind him, you can feel the heat of Professional Lady's gaze.

"Think of this"—you indicate the group behind you—"as a line of gunpowder, waiting for a spark to touch it off." You gesture at the old man who is staring at you with a puzzled expression. "Are you going to let him be your spark?"

"Are you hitting on me?" the old man says.

"No," you tell him.

The Go-Go Executive explodes. "Oh, for fu—"

"All right!" The shift manager waggles a finger at the barista. "Override that order," they shriek. "Override them all!"

Spontaneous applause breaks out, and the shift manager's face goes from beet red to charmingly pink to unnaturally pale. You can tell they just did the math. Sure, their CPH is going to go back up, but their sales per hour metric has tanked. That's going to be a problem with Corporate. They may not know why—Corporate never looks at anything beyond the high level summary of each region—but they're going to see a weird glitch in the graph. That's going to draw their attention.

For a moment, you feel sorry for the shift manager. Having the vast, unblinking attention of a soulless entity focus on you is not a fun feeling. But you can't help them. Corporate is not a cosmic intelligence indifferent to the fate of humanity. They are a monstrous byproduct of a commodities-driven, capitalist-slave dialectic, which is to say a product of our own psychoses. The Night Office can't fix those.

THIS HAS BEEN A NON-SCORING EDUCATIONAL ASSESSMENT EXERCISE. THE NIGHT OFFICE ACKNOWLEDES YOUR ABILITY TO MANIPULATE MIDDLE MANAGEMENT.

DON'T PAT YOURSELF ON THE BACK TOO HARD, THOUGH.

MIDDLE MANAGEMENT FRIGHTENS READILY AND IS EASY TO COERCE.

WE MENTIONED A COMPLIMENTARY COFFEE VOUCHER, BUT WE SUSPECT YOUR VIEW OF DEEPLY COMMODITIZED FRANCHISE COFFEE SHOPS HAS CHANGED.

No, actually, it hasn't. A voucher is a voucher.
Go to 62.

25

They ran out of soup an hour ago. But thinking outside the box is a personality quirk the Night Office likes to encourage.

In the interim, it looks like that old guy has finally managed to finish his order with the barista. He's moving on. Watch Guy is now stepping up to place his order. He rattles off his beverage of choice, and wow, it sounds complicated.

How does this make you feel?
Go to 30.

The barista is good. She doesn't bat an eye at his precise directions. Isn't it marvelous how idiosyncratic the coffee-ordering process is?
Go to 31.

26

Tweaker has a Hand of Glory.

Now, in the traditional literature, a Hand of Glory (which is the mummified hand—preferably the left one—of a man who has been hanged) is used to render people motionless. Typically, you shove a candle between a couple of the fingers, light it, and when you wave it around, anyone caught in the light's embrace is put on hold.

No, we're not going to share the recipe for making one of these. There are a number of existing manuscripts that detail the making of a Hand of Glory. Do your own damn research.

Anyway, the hand that Tweaker is waving about is not that sort of Hand of Glory. This hand is used for Opening.

Every Night Office field team is comprised of three individuals: an Opener, a Guide, and a Closer. Each of these individuals have specific talents, and these talents require specific tools. Closers get their coats of many pockets. Openers get their Hand. We're not going to talk about Guides, because you haven't signed enough non-disclosure agreements.

An Opener's Hand is an apparatus that augments their living flesh. They use it to open things: doors, chests, safes, portals to other dimensions. There are rules, of course, and most of them are governed by the basic formulas of sympathetic magic.

Anyway, Tweaker is using a homemade substitute. Not as good as the real thing, but functional enough. Using the Hand of Glory, he's going to Open a gate, and through that gate are going to come a bunch of slobbering slouchers with too many mouths.

Go to 28.

27

The old man looks at you like you've got a eye growing on a stalk in the center of your forehead.

"It's a voucher," you explain. "It'll pay for your coffee."

The crew member behind the counter examines the metaphysical voucher in your hand. "Actually," they say, "it'll only pay for part of it."

"What?"

"His Supra Mocha Hazelnut Deluxe Whip Double Double is $7.56," the crew member says.

"Is that what you ordered?" You ask the old man.

He shrugs. He can't remember.

Your voucher won't even pay for half. It's a gesture, all right, and not much else. You still need to come up with another $4.56.

Help the old man check his pockets.
Go to 51.

Ask the dude with the expensive watch and the high blood pressure if he can spare you a fiver.
Go to 52.

28

Tweaker waves his special hand at the nearest person, which happens to be Exercise Grandma. She may look like she's a vacuous socialite who has never worked an honest day's work in the last half-century, but here are two things you don't know about her: she ran two marathons last year; and, over a eight year period starting when she was seventeen, she naturally birthed six daughters. This woman knows something about pain.

She's also doesn't like arrogant men who don't respect women (like that idiot with the watch in line ahead of you), and when Tweaker starts swearing and waving mummified body parts at her, well, she's not having any of that.

"Point that thing somewhere else," she snaps at him.

He gets in close, jabbing the hand at her face.

Now, in addition to having core muscles denser than a failing star and the wiry musculature of a person capable of outrunning a forest fire or an incoming tsunami, Exercise Grandma has been studying Jeet Kune Do for longer than Tweaker has been alive. And so, the third time Tweaker's mummy hand comes at her, Exercise Grandma responds.

The glass in the display case cracks as Tweaker's head rebounds off it. He sags to his knees and then collapses on his face.

You didn't even see what Exercise Grandma did. She's fast.

Tweaker dropped the Hand of Glory. It's right over there, lying on the floor. Are you going to pick it up?

Better you than someone else.
Go to 49.

There's no way in hell you're going to touch that thing.
Go to 48.

29

Yes, there's a guy in a hoodie in line with you. Do you not remember him from the original line-up? Seriously? Do you need a recap?

Fine. There's the old dude, who is standing over in the corner now, staring vacantly at the community bulletin board. Supra Mocha Whatever Whatever Double Stuff guy is over at the end of the counter, checking his watch and vibrating. Behind you is Exercise Grandma, who may or may not be someone else entirely, but let's not get distracted by inconsequential minutia (once an exercise is enough, frankly). Behind her is the guy in the hoodie, who looks like he spends most of his days (and nights, most likely) tweaking out on whatever cheap chemical stimulant he can score. Behind him is—oh, wait. Tweaker can't hold it in any more.

"Alpha. Dogma. Dark beans of Betelguese, I summon thee!"

He pulls something out of the front pocket of his hoodie and starts waving it around.

Of course, his pants are in danger of crowding his ankles since he's busy waving . . . whatever that thing in his hand is. It would be comical to watch, if it weren't for the fact that he's babbling on about "blood and souls," like he's trying out for the role of Necromantic Master of the Darkest Arts for a local RenFaire stage production.

You'd better do something soon.

Shove Exercise Grandma at him.
Go to 39.

Vault over the counter.
Go to 40.

30

Your emotional reaction to events—whether they are explicitly relevant to an investigation or not—impacts your performance as a Night Office field operative. If you are easily annoyed or perturbed by strong personality types, you may have difficulties interacting with local law enforcement officers, sanctimonious city officials, arrogant government agents from three-lettered acronym agencies, and overly suspicious sanitation workers. If you are easily cowed by these folks, you're not going to be able to command a scene.

Somewhat tangentially, your ability to sit through a meandering mental exercise that might not have any payoff whatsoever is also part of our assessment as to your viability as a potential candidate for a Night Office field operative position. It's all useful data for us. We wouldn't want you to think we were *that* mean-spirited and sadistic.

Check here to acknowledge you have read and understood the baseline data collection aspect of this assessment.
Go to 45.

Check here to acknowledge you find this sort of mental manipulation tedious and too much like that relationship you had with that self-described tennis "pro" about two years ago. He was an abusive jackass.
Go to 37.

31

It certainly is nice that everyone can order exactly the sort of beverage they want, isn't it? Though, to be fair, all of these complicated personalized variants are merely a granularity of pre-processed additives that don't really change the fundamental nature of the core consumable. Whether you get three pumps of white chocolate or two and a half squirts of pumpkin spice mix, it's still coffee.

That said, Watch Guy is a Supra Mocha Hazelnut Deluxe Whip Double Double sort of guy. You're not entirely sure what the "Double Double" part of the beverage actually is, and you'd be willing to bet he doesn't either, but he's not going to admit it. It's all part of his persona at this point. He's a Supra Double Double sort of fellow.

Judging by the barista's lack of expression and her quick *tap-tap-tap* of the register, she's got her own opinion of this guy. Spoiler: it's not high. She's more interested in the guy wearing the hoodie.

Oh, did you forget about him?

Oh, dear. That may have been a mistake.
Go to 46.

There's a guy wearing a hoodie?
Go to 29.

32

One of the often-overused descriptive phrases is this business is "non-Euclidean geometry." Sure, it's the sort of linguistic bibble-babble pulp authors use to give their narratives a decidedly exotic feel. But it is also shorthand for "this is some weird shit the human language doesn't encompass very well."

Which is to say: you'll hear the phrase quite often as a Night Office field operative. If you're the type of person who gets hung up on the "rules," well, we have some news for you.

The rules are non-Platonic, non-Aristotelian, and definitely non-Descartian. They follow the nightmare logic of a collaboration between Salvador Dali and M. C. Escher. You'll have more luck understanding the multiplicity algorithm that fractures synthetic collateralized debt obligations.

Once you finish your Orientation and Inoculation, you will have a better understanding of the *spirit* of the rules. Many field operatives leave the Night Office without ever understanding the letter of the rules. It is, in fact, quite likely that you will perish while serving as a Night Office field operative with no more understanding of what the hell is going on than you have right now.

We're not telling this in an effort to put you off on your dream of becoming a Night Office field operative, but to assist you in setting your expectations accordingly.

Wasn't that helpful?

Not really.
Go to 37.

Barely, but what choice you do have?
Go to 38.

33

You didn't send all those sex toys to your apartment, did you?

What? Was that wrong?
Go to 34.

Of course not. They weren't for you, anyway.
Go to 36.

34

Now we understand why you yelled "dildo" earlier. It's interesting what these psychological assessment exercises reveal about the people who are taking them. Fascinating stuff.

Never mind that. Shouldn't we focus on the exercise?
Go to 14.

Oh, you thought *you* were taking this test? No, this test is taking *you*. Clever, aren't we?
Go to 37.

35

As Tweaker is waving the hand around, a look of glazed triumph on his face, you make eye contact with Professional Lady standing behind him. She sees you looking at her, and there's something in your expression that connects with her. She stands a little straighter, a tiny shiver running up her back.

"Abjuration Contemplation," Tweaker beings. "I offer thee—"

This is as far as he gets. Professional Lady, having been acknowledged as a professional by your glance, pulls a heavy revolver out of her coat. She doesn't bother pointing it at Tweaker. She merely grabs it by the barrel and brings the butt of the weapon down on Tweaker's head.

He makes a funny noise, sort of like the sound a ground hog would make as it was being sucked into vacuum cleaner, and his eyes roll back in his head.

Professional Lady, continuing to be exceptionally professional, hits him again. There's a little blood spatter this time, and Tweaker drops like a sack full of anesthetized kittens. He even mewls a little as he sprawls on the floor.

The Hand of Glory tumbles out of his hand.

You and Professional Lady look at the hand, and then look at one another.

"Good work," you say.
Go to 56.

"I'll take that," you say, nodding at the Hand of Glory.
Go to 50.

36

The sex toys weren't for you? Oh, okay. No, we're not judging. In some counties, these sorts of things are still legal, so you're— hey, it's all cool. Don't get worked up about it.

It's important to stay focused when you are on job. You can't get distracted by past aggressions that you haven't let go, or misdirected creative energies, or why that shipment from that *special* shop is late. You have to pay attention to your surroundings. You to be present, in the now. Stop day-dreaming already.

Anyway, Hoodie Guy is waving something around. It's not a dildo—stop thinking like that. It's a severed hand, which is . . . better?

Is that better?

Look: the only reason to have a dead man's hand is if you are planning on opening something that shouldn't be opened. This kid a rogue opener. Is he operating under his own volition? Is he under the influence of some malevolent agency? What sort of terrifying brain-sucking monstrosities does he hope to summon?

Oh, right. You're not supposed to be here. You were just killing some time before an interview (oh, such a dangerous pastime, don't you think?). You're totally not trained for this sort of nonsense.

And yet, here you are. Shit's about to get weird. Are you ready to do what needs to be done?

You are ready. Let's go!
Go to 37.

Oh, you have some more questions?
Go to 38.

37

Congratulations. You have discerned the true nature of this exercise. The Night Office is pleased with your ability to focus, ignore distractions, and plot a viable solution in an environment that appears meaningless, inconsequential, and surreal.

Or, as field operatives like to say: "Monday."

THIS IS A NON-SCORING EDUCATIONAL ASSESSMENT EXPERIENCE. HOWEVER, WE ARE PLEASED TO OFFER YOU A COMPLIMENTARY COFFEE VOUCHER.

Go to 62 for your voucher.

38

It's nice that you have more questions. It shows a willingness to push back against authority. That's adorable. Okay, we'll play along. Here we go:

a) Night Office field operatives act on their own initiation, direction, and discernment. They do not answer to any higher authority on this temporal sphere. It's nice if you can manage to follow the chain of command within the organization, of course, but decisions on the ground take priority over some nozzle-head trying to quarterback you from the security of a Farraday Office back at HQ.

b) That said, most often than not, you won't have a clue as to the big picture. If you survive long enough, you may begin to perceive the shadow cast by the various tentacles of the vast cosmic conspiracy. But don't hold your breath.

c) This also extends to the inner workings of the Night Office. You may have some insight into how a minor part of the Cosmic Body works, but you're never going to be invited to sit at the head table and talk shop about the Great Plan. Don't expect to be told anything. Don't expect to understand anything. Do your job. Go home at the end of the day. Don't fret the rest of it.

Seriously. It's better this way. Trust us.

d) No one knows how the Universe works. Get over it already. Have your questions be satisfactorily answered?

Yes. No? Sort of?
Go to 14.

Not in the slightest.
Go to 37.

39

You push Exercise Grandma at Tweaker.

If this action leads to a successful conclusion of this educational assessment exercise, then it was the proper action to take. We are not judging you. It is, however, a bit unorthodox, but unorthodox thinking can be the sort of thinking that saves the Universe. Your willingness to commit to these modes are thought are commendable, and they are the salt of every successful Night Office field operative.

You won't get invited to many cocktail parties because other people are going to find you a bit . . . *unorthodox*. We are confident you can manage the emotional toll of this sort of estrangement from casual society.

Anyway, Exercise Grandma pinwheels her arms and makes an outraged chicken noise. Tweaker is perplexed by the love attack this septuagenarian is bringing. He bats at her with the mummified hand and manages to get it tangled with her highly stylized and heavily sculpted hairdo.

While these two are busy shrieking and flailing at one another, Professional Lady, who has been watching all of this with a look of utter contempt written all over her face, rummages in her purse and finds a gold-plated Zippo. She flicks it open, scratches the wheel with a calloused thumb, and a six inch flame shoots up. She steps forward and applies the flame to the back of Exercise Grandma's hair.

Exercise Grandma's hair ignites. The Hand of Glory (which is equally pickled) bursts into flame as well. Professional Lady snatches the flaming wand from Tweaker's slack grasp, pokes him in the eye with a fiery digit, and then beats the hand against the glass display case, scattering flaming bits of mummified flesh, until the old bones break.

The world having been saved, Professional Lady drops the ruined hand, straightens her blazer, and says in perfectly modulated voice. "There. We're all safe now. Can I get a fucking coffee?"

Behind her, Tweaker and Exercise Grandma writhe on the floor, trying to put out the multi-hued flames that are devouring their brains.

One of the baristas starts to clap, but she is shushed by the shift manager.

Distantly, you hear someone trying to explain to a 911 operator what just happened.

Professional Lady is looking at you, one eyebrow cocked.

You give her a thumbs-up.

THIS HAS BEEN A NON-SCORING EDUCATIONAL EXERCISE. WE HOPE IT HAS BEEN AN EXCITING OPPORTUNITY TO LEARN MORE ABOUT THE NIGHT OFFICE.

WE'D LIKE TO OFFER YOU A COMPLIMENTARY COFFEE VOUCHER.

Go to 62.

40

You attempt to vault over the counter, which would be difficult even if there weren't two cash registers and a half-dozen display racks filled with all manner of last-minute treat options.

However, let's give you the benefit of the doubt. Perhaps you were a fine juvenile delinquent and got lots of practice hopping and climbing over barriers meant to keep out miscreants like yourself. So, yes, you brace yourself with one hand, throw up a leg, and give yourself a heave and a ho.

Have you not been paying attention to how many crew members are behind the counter? Or the shift manager, who has been standing right there this whole time. You may have thought their job was to get in the way of all the crew members, but actually, they are standing there solely for the purpose of confounding your attempt at being clever. Because, let's be honest, since this shift manager isn't self-aware enough to realize how much of an obstruction they are to the smooth operation of this coffee shop, they certainly aren't going to suddenly hop out of the way when you need to get by.

We'll grant you the experience and expertise to hop the counter, but we've got a flabby career executive with no hope for corporate advancement as a secondary obstacle.

It's the secondary obstacles that always get you.

You and the shift manager tango, and it's a lovely tango, but doing so takes five or eight seconds, which is four seconds longer than it takes Tweaker to open the gate to the Nether Underbelly of Shaggnurroth's Decaying Corpse, which is where the gluttonous corpse crawlers of Tzadderach have been feeding for the last millennia.

The appetites of these creatures are endless, which is why the bloated corpse of a sky god was a good place to stick them. It would take them nearly a hundred million years to devour all of Shaggnurroth, during which time, the crawlers would never stop and think: "Hello. I wonder if there is more to life than gnawing on the gristly bits of this near-petrified cosmic deity?"

However, the scent of living flesh—especially living flesh that has been lightly toasted—is like ambrosia to an endless voracious corpse crawler of Tzadderach. Which means these nasty biters are now falling through the gate that Tweaker's Hand of Glory has opened, and they are eagerly trying to bite everyone who is still in the coffee shop.

As you can imagine, this doesn't end well for a lot of folks.

THIS HAS BEEN A NON-SCORING EDUCATIONAL ASSESSMENT EXERCISE. WE HOPED IT WAS USEFUL TO YOU. FOR THE RECORD, THE NIGHT OFFICE IS NOT LIABLE FOR ANY EMOTIONAL DURESS YOU MIGHT LATER EXHIBIT AS A RESULT OF PARTICIPATING IN THIS EDUCATIONAL ASSESSMENT EXERCISE.

PLEASE ACCEPT A COMPLIMENTARY COFFEE VOUCHER AS COMPENSATION FOR YOUR TIME.

Go to 62.

41

Exercise Grandma was playing dead. Does that make you feel better now?

Of course, Exercise Grandma didn't care for you kicking her in the ribs to see if she's still alive. She's yelling at you and waving her hand in your face. Her knuckles have been ravaged by arthritis over the years, and so her extended finger has a crook in the last digit that make it look like a hook. As in, she is going to shove that finger in your eye socket and hook it around. Talk about being led by your nose.

Anyway, all of this nonsense means you're distracted from what Tweaker is doing with the Hand of Glory.

What's a Hand of Glory for? Oh, it's for Opening.

Tweaker's got some friends, apparently. They're on the other side of a cosmic gate, and they're eager to come over and play. There's a lot of fear and panic in the air, and Tweaker's pals can smell that stink, even on the other side of that inter-dimensional portal. When Tweaker bangs that mummified hand on the display glass three times, the wall behind the counter melts.

Things come through.

What sort of things? Oh, we can't tell you, for two reasons: 1) You haven't signed the appropriate documentation for access to this sort of information; and 2) The descriptions alone will drive you insane. The Night Office offers a comprehensive Orientation and Inoculation Program that will prepare you for dealing with cosmic horrors from outer space.

Regardless, these indescribable things use their [**REDACTED**] to tear people apart. Things get messy. Eventually, they [**REDACTED**] to you.

It really hurts for a second, and then you don't feel anything ever again.

CONGRATULATIONS. YOU HAVE REACHED THE END OF THIS NON-SCORING EDUCATIONAL ASSESSMENT EXPERIENCE.

WE DID PROMISE YOU A COMPLIMENTARY COFFEE VOUCHER.

Go to 62 for your voucher.

42

The crew member at the counter pushes buttons on their register and a total flashes on the screen. $8.75.

You only have a $3 voucher (and it's not even a real voucher). You're now holding up the line. Funny how that happens.

The shift manager, who has been hovering in the background in a way that maximizes the stress of the baristas hurrying back and forth in the work area, pushes themselves toward the front counter. "Is there an issue here?" they ask nervously.

"I forgot my wallet, but I have this voucher," you say. You show them the voucher.

The shift manager pales. "You—" they start. They look at the people in line behind you. "They—" A barista with their hands full of frosted beverages can't squeeze past the shift manager. "We—" the shift manager says.

"Is there a problem?" you ask.

The shift manager swallows some spit, makes a face at the taste, and then jerks their head toward the end of counter. You extricate yourself from the line, much to everyone's relief.

At the end of the counter, the shift manager pushes through a swinging door. After a moment's hesitation, you follow.

The back is a cramped office space with a number of metal racks filled with a variety of packaged products necessary for the successful operation of a coffee shop.

None of these products are coffee, by the way.

The shift manager takes down a framed certificate (it says that this store won some kind of regional award last year), and behind the frame, there is a flat panel with a thin slot below it. "There," the shift manager says, pointing at the slot.

You offer the shift manager the voucher, but they won't touch it, and so you carefully feed the end of the voucher into the slot beneath the panel. A machine wakes up in the wall, and the voucher is sucked out of your grip.

Something makes a *bing!* noise, and the flat panel slides open. A light comes on, illuminating a surprisingly deep cavity. The only thing in the wall safe is a leather bag.

You notice that the shift manager has fled the storeroom. You're all alone back here.

There can't be anything good in that bag.

Take it anyway.
Go to 63.

Leave it alone.
Go to 65.

43

Look, just admit you're not keen on having to decide which of the five people in line with you is possessed by a space jelly. You have a terrible time reading people. You don't like the inane break room talk that goes on at work. All you want is to be left alone in your cubicle where you can talk to the numbers on your screen. The numbers don't have ulterior motives. The numbers don't laugh at you behind your back. The numbers don't edge away from you in the elevator.

It's okay. We understand. You'll find there are many like you in the Night Office. The Night Office does not hire individuals who require constant social attention. They are not in the business of building relationship networks. At the Night Office, you can show up, rotate into an assignment, complete that assignment, and go home without talking to more than one other person. In the privacy of your own home, you can drink straight from the bottle. You can eat right out of the microwave tray with a plastic fork while standing at the sink. You can wear your favorite latex pajamas and tighten those hand-made clamps all you like. The Night Office doesn't even care what you watch on the flickering idiot box while you do so. Just make sure you don't alarm the neighbors with weird smells or strange noises, and show up on time for your shift.

It's going to be okay. Deep breath. This is just a test. You're not going to be asked to put an eight hundred kilogram feral octopus with poison suckers into a lead-lined shoe box.

Not this week, at any rate.

The point is: it's okay if you prefer to get a sandwich (the pot-roasted pork is really good, by the way) and a cold beverage instead of facing eldritch horrors that want to suck the skin off your body. The Night Office understands. In fact, the Night

Office prefers to know this now instead of after we've starting paperwork on your behalf.

What's it going to be?

The sandwich and a sparkling water.
Go to 44.

Get back into this. The world needs saving!
Go to 45.

44

The crew member smiles. "Excellent choice," they say.

You get the sense that's a scripted response. A little part of you die at the thought that this person spends their entire day telling people that they've made an excellent choice when it really doesn't matter what they pick. Their whole existence is spent affirming a valueless decision. Can you imagine the effect that has on their self-confidence? At the end of their shift, the shift manager probably says to them: "Excellent work today, crew member #33566-A."

And this crew member knows the sentiment proffered by their shift manager is just as empty and meaningless as their scripted response at the counter. How does this crew member feel about their work? How will this realization affect their ability to perform their scripted duty tomorrow? Will there be a quaver in their voice after the thirteenth or twenty-third customer tomorrow?

Will the shift manager—who is constantly hovering in the background, doing nothing useful, but who is definitely getting in the way of crew members who are actively trying to do their menial jobs—will this manager hear the tremor in their employee's voice and think: "Am I not doing enough to support them? Are they going to fail at this task? Will a customer leave a four-star review for this coffee shop, thereby destroying any chance I might have at becoming district manager?"

So many questions. But don't worry about them. They'll be fine. You've got your sandwich and fizzy water. You're good.

THIS HAS BEEN A NON-SCORING EDUCATIONAL ASSESSMENT EXERCISE.

WE MENTIONED A COMPLIMENTARY COFFEE VOUCHER EARLIER, BUT… LOOK, WHILE WE SAID IT WAS A "NON-SCORING" ASSESSMENT, WE WERE TOTALLY JUDGING YOU.

AFTER ALL, YOU BOUGHT A SANDWICH INSTEAD OF FACING TENTACLED DOOM FROM DEEP SPACE. WHILE WE DON'T BLAME YOU FOR PICKING THE SAFE SOLUTION IN THIS EXERCISE, WE ARE A LITTLE DISAPPOINTED BY YOUR LACK OF INITIATIVE. AND SO, YES, WE'RE GOING TO BE PETTY AND NOT GIVE YOU THAT VOUCHER.

IT'S A LIFE LESSON, REALLY. DON'T GET ALL WORKED UP ABOUT IT.

OKAY, FINE. IF YOU WANT TO START OVER, YOU CAN. (IN FACT, LOOK OVER AT THE OPPOSITE PAGE!)

DON'T END UP HERE A SECOND TIME, THOUGH. THERE WILL BE NO AVOIDING OUR JUDGMENT THEN.

45

Right, back to the coffee shop. Good for you.

You're in line. There's an old man at the counter. He can't follow the menus. His frustration is mounting.

Behind him is a man dressed in a suit too expensive for his income bracket, but we can't shame him for trying to visualize the person he wants to be. He looks at his very fancy watch often, not because he's pressed for time, but because he wants everyone in the coffee shop to notice his shiny status symbol.

You're next in line, eager to tackle this exercise again. Excellent. This sort of enthusiasm is noted.

Behind you is Exercise Grandma, who—for the record—isn't a very good grandmother, nor does she exercise as much as her attire would want you to believe.

Behind her is Tweaker. Hey, here's a little secret: Tweaker has a Hand of Glory in the front pocket of his hoodie. He's going to lose his shit in a few seconds and open a gate to Shard-Zazz-Xun, where creatures with tentacles and pincers are waiting.

Shhh. Don't spoil it for him. He's been waiting a long time for this moment.

Anyway, behind him is a professional looking woman in a severe business suit and a more severe haircut. She might look like she's in charge, but in actuality, no one ever lets her run meetings and she's perpetually pissed about it.

Now, what do you do?

Wait for Tweaker to make his move.
Go to 46.

Make eye contact with the professional lady at the back.
Go to 35.

46

The greasy fellow in line behind you ("Tweaker" to his case officers) fumbles with something in the pocket of his hoodie. It could be many things—a wallet, a small emotional support puppy, a loaf of bread, a gun—but it's none of those things. It's not even a pink dildo.

It's a mummified hand.

A what?
Go to 26.

You don't have to know what that is to know that it means trouble.
Go to 28.

47

"You're not going to shoot me," you say to the Professional Lady.

She raises an eyebrow. "I've had a trying week," she says. The barrel of her revolver doesn't waver.

"Think of the paperwork," you say. You take one step toward the Hand of Glory.

"Think of the hole in your head," she snaps back.

You shake your head. "It'll be quiet," you tell her. "Quiet and peaceful." You take another step.

Her aim wavers.

You glance down at the Hand of Glory. Two more steps. You're almost there.

You look at Professional Lady again. Her eyes are bright now. There's a tiny tremor in her hand.

"I haven't had a day off in sixteen weeks," you tell her. "My kids keep forgetting my name. I've forgotten my own name a couple of times." You shrug. "You'll remember my name, though, won't you? After all, it'll be linked to yours forever if you pull that trigger."

She's on the edge. It won't take much to push her either way. It'll take a deft touch to pull this off.

You take one more step.

"It'll be nice to be remembered," you say.

She starts to cry.

You take one more step. She doesn't shoot you.

The Hand of Glory is yours.

THIS HAS BEEN A NON-SCORING EDUCATIONAL ASSESSMENT EXERCISE.

YOU DID WELL, THOUGH WE PREFER THAT NIGHT OFFICE FIELD OPERATIVES DON'T FORGE EMOTIONAL BONDS WITH

CIVILIANS. RELATIONSHIPS WHICH ARISE FROM THESE SORTS OF CIRCUMSTANCES NEVER LAST.

HOWEVER, WE DO HAVE A COMPLIMENTARY COFFEE VOUCHER WE WOULD LIKE TO OFFER YOU. THAT'S ABOUT AS MUCH EMOTIONAL ATTACHMENT AS YOU SHOULD HAVE FOR ANYTHING OR ANYONE AS A NIGHT OFFICE FIELD OPERATIVE.

Go to 62.

48

If you're not going to pick up the Hand of Glory, who is? Do you trust anyone else in this coffee shop with a Relic of Opening? Look how easy it was for Tweaker to nearly bring about the end of all human existence.

Okay, so he'd been practicing with it for a few weeks, and he was under the influence of eldritch narcotics that made him susceptible to temporal harmonic suggestions from the fourth planet in the Calderon Prime system. But let's not get lost in the weeds here.

The point is: it's a mystical artifact, and you're the closest thing to an expert in this coffee shop. What are you going to do?

Fine. Pick up the relic.
Go to 59.

You're going to continue to *not* touch the damn thing is what you're going to do.
Go to 53.

49

Displaying more confidence than you feel, you pick up the Hand of Glory. It has an odd smell to it. Sort of how your grandma used to smell. You remember visiting her at that old house on Marbleview Lane. It was always overcast on that narrow street, and the wind would whistle through the ragged trees, taunting you like a creepy old man with a stained paper bag of slimy candy. Grandma didn't like to wear her teeth, and her robe would gape at awkward moments. She liked to talk about the war, though you never found out which war.

You brought her lemon cake, which she always devoured without bothering with a fork or plate. She liked you.

You still miss her every once in a while.

Anyway, you've got the Hand of Glory now. Well done. Make sure you turn that in. We wouldn't want you keeping a souvenir or anything . . .

THIS HAS BEEN A NON-SCORING EDUCATIONAL ASSESSMENT EXERCISE. YOU HAVE DEMONSTRATED MENTAL ACUITY, FORE-THOUGHT, AND A REASONABLE ABILITY TO TROUBLESHOOT REAL-WORLD PROBLEMS. THE NIGHT OFFICE APPRECIATES THIS OPPORTUNITY TO EXAMINE YOU.

IN CONSIDERATION OF YOUR TIME, THE NIGHT OFFICE WOULD LIKE TO OFFER YOU A COMPLIMENTARY COFFEE VOUCHER.

Go to 62.

50

Professional Lady is ready for that sort of nonsense from you. She swings the revolver around in her hand (more of a finger twirl than a full-hand gesture, if you really want to know), and as you reach for the Hand, you hear the ominous sound of the revolver's hammer going back.

"I don't think so," Professional Lady says.

Call her bluff?
Go to 47.

Hey, she's the professional here.
Go to 57.

51

You get up close to the old man, and the pair of you dance around who gets to put their hands in his pockets. He seems befuddled by the whole idea of you pocket frisking him. You notice a lot of people are staring at you.

Well, except from the dude in the hoodie. He seems to be interested in a spot on the far wall.

Anyway, you shove both of your hands in the old man's front pockets and start rooting around.

It's incredibly awkward, especially as the pockets seem deeper than they should be. Your left hand encounters something, but it . . . that's weird. It felt like whatever you touched wiggled away from you.

The old man starts chuckling. "What's so funny?" you demand, your face flushing with embarrassment about this whole thing.

"I'm going to eat your brains," the old man says. He grins, and his smile gets bigger than his face allows.

You try to pull your hands out of his pockets, but before you can yank them free, something grabs them. That's right. Your hands are grabbed by other hands! Hands within the old man's pockets. What the hell?

They've got a real good grip on you too.

As you struggle to pull away from the old man, the top half of his head tilts back, exposing a giant mouth with a dark throat and a rim of incredibly sharp teeth. He says something, but his mouth is so distorted you can make out his words. You get the idea, however.

The hands holding your hands jerk downward, pulling your torso forward. The crown of your head is exposed.

Oh, this is a terrible way to go . . .

THIS HAS BEEN A NON-SCORING EDUCATIONAL ASSESSMENT EXERCISE.

WE MENTIONED A COMPLIMENTARY COFFEE VOUCHER EARLIER, BUT SINCE YOUR HEAD HAS JUST BEEN EATEN BY A SBARRILIAN SHARK-IN-WAITING, WE'RE NOT QUITE SURE HOW YOU'RE GOING TO DRINK THE COFFEE.

52

The tightly wound executive salesman of the nearby Autorama Sell-n-Go does not have time for charity. He needs sixteen ounces of pure cocaine—sorry, caffeine—coursing through his veins right now. You giving him the big puppy dog eyes about helping an old man out is increasing his already alarmingly high blood pressure.

"It's just five—" you start.

The salesman checks his watch. It's more important than anything you might have to say.

Ignore him. He's the sort who wouldn't haul you out of a burning building, even if you promised him you'd come test drive the latest SUV model.

Go to 24.

How's your blood pressure? It's elevated, isn't it? Slapping the shit out of this dude would definitely reduce your stress levels, wouldn't it?

Go to 58.

53

Your prudence and restraint is noted. However, someone needs to do something about that Hand of Glory. You can't leave it lying in the middle of the coffee shop like that.

You beg to differ. It looks fine where it is.
Go to 60.

Oh, okay. Maybe you should pick it up.
Go to 59.

54

Let's face it. You're a mess. You're constantly second-guessing yourself. Is "Hoodie Guy" better than "Tweaker"? It doesn't sound like it. "Hoodie Guy" sounds like you picked the romantic comedy thread, whereas "Tweaker" sounds like the thread where things were going to get interesting.

(To be fair, you're not wrong.)

Does that mean you failed already? How useful of an assessment is a thread where the narrative is merely whether or not Hoodie Guy manages to ask Sulty Barista for her phone number? What does that tell anyone about your ability to navigate a tortuous minefield of complex psychological choices?

Well, it tells us a great deal, in fact, because people are hard. Sometimes it's not about monsters with eyes on the insides of their mouths (so they can watch you be crushed by their jagged teeth). Sometimes it's about love and affection and making a real connection with another human being.

Look, empathy isn't required, but it certainly helps.

Not every story is a horror story.

Though that doesn't mean you should let your guard down . . .

THIS IS A NON-SCORING EDUCATIONAL ASSESSMENT EXERCISE. IT MAY FEEL UNREWARDING IN ITS PRESENT CONCLUSION, BUT CLOSURE IS RARELY SOMETHING YOU GET WITH THE NIGHT OFFICE.

HOWEVER, THAT COMPLIMENTARY VOUCHER OFFER IS STILL GOOD, SO YOU HAVE THAT COMING TO YOU.

Go to 62.

55

Apparently, this exercise is offering too many side paths, red herrings, and dead ends for your liking. The Night Office would like to assure you that it is entirely sympathetic to your infantile needs for immediate gratification and puerile entertainment. The Night Office understands that nuance is not required in the slash-and-burn methodology of modern corporate malfeasance. Caring about puppies and other humans is for the weak. The Night Office is aware of this mindset. They see it every day, mostly in the drool-flecked visages of fools who have been tempted by illusory promises made by sadistic minions of cosmic intelligences whose eternal boredom are barely impacted by the existential subjugation of entire species.

Which is to say, if you can't be bothered to notice the needs of other human beings, how can you stand firm when asked why you are defending these poor saps?

Food for thought.

The ridiculous drink order is actually for that asshat with the expensive watch standing behind you. The old man ordered a small cappuccino, mostly dry.

When the barista puts it on the counter for him, he offers to split it with you.

How do you feel about yourself now?

THIS IS A NON-SCORING EDUCATIONAL ASSESSMENT EXERCISE. SINCE YOU USED THE COMPLIMENTARY COFFEE VOUCHER AS PART OF THIS EXERCISE, WE CAN NO LONGER OFFER IT TO YOU.

HOWEVER, WE MIGHT HAVE GIVEN YOU SOMETHING MUCH BETTER. THINK ABOUT IT.

56

"Of course," the Professional Lady says. "It's what I do."

She walks over, picks up the Hand of Glory, and tucks it into her coat. You're not quite sure how it fits, but there's no bulge in her jacket. You're still puzzling over that bit of fashion physics as she walks out of the coffee shop.

After a few moments, the line reforms and everyone gets on with their day. Except those who can't, of course. But the line will work around them easily enough. It's not the first time this sort of thing has happened here.

THIS HAS BEEN A NON-SCORING EDUCATIONAL ASSESSMENT EXERCISE. THANK YOU FOR YOUR PARTICIPATION.

WE'D LIKE TO OFFER YOU A COMPLIMENTARY COFFEE VOUCHER.

Go to 62.

57

You back away from the Hand of Glory, keeping your hands in plain sight. The Professional Lady slips her gun back into her coat. You're not sure where it goes. It's a bit puzzling, in fact.

She walks over to the Hand, and produces a heavy-duty plastic sack from an outer pocket of her coat. She wraps the bag around the Hand, and then slips both into an inner pocket of her coat.

You stare at the coat. There should be a large bulge on the left side. The Hand should distress the line of the fabric, but the coat looks immaculate. It drapes in a very pleasing fashion.

Professional Lady sees your frown. She puts a finger to her lips, hiding a smile. Without another word, she leaves.

Tweaker continues to lie on the floor. He twitches now and again. It looks like the bleeding on his head has stopped.

Behind you, Executive Asshole is loudly ordering some kind of coffee beverage that has at least eight modifiers to it.

Exercise Grandma looks up from her phone, notices Tweaker on the floor, and then goes back to her phone.

You start to wonder if you imagined the Professional Lady, but you fight that thought because you know that's exactly what she wants you to think.

THIS HAS BEEN A NON-SCORING EDUCATIONAL ASSESSMENT EXERCISE. SOME OF YOUR MISSIONS WILL END LIKE THIS. IT'S OKAY. THE WORLD IS SAVED. THAT IS ALL THAT MATTERS.

TO CELEBRATE, THE NIGHT OFFICE WOULD LIKE TO OFFER YOU A COMPLIMENTARY COFFEE VOUCHER.

Go to 62.

58

The Night Office does not condone physical assault on a Self-Absorbed Narcissist, Unclassified (SANU). Not because there might be lawsuits, but because it means you aren't paying attention to the imminent threat in your immediate area. If you spend all your time slapping the idiots who can't be bothered to realize they're about to be turned into mindless chattel of a trans-dimensional slobbering thing, you'll never get anything done. So, yes, you could slap this idiot, but while you're doing that (and enjoying the smug satisfaction of doing so), it is likely you're going to miss the critical event that will precipitate the end of the world.

Try to focus better next time.

THIS HAS BEEN A NON-SCORING EDUCATIONAL ASSESSMENT EXERCISE. WE HOPE YOU HAVE LEARNED SOMETHING ABOUT WHAT IS TRULY IMPORTANT.

WE'D LIKE TO OFFER YOU A COMPLIMENTARY COFFEE VOUCHER, WHICH SHOULD NOT BE READ AS CONDONING PHYSICAL ASSAULT AS A MEANS TO AN END. THE NIGHT OFFICE HAS NOT REWARDED SUCH ACTIONS FOR QUITE SOME TIME. LAWSUITS NOTWITHSTANDING.

Go to 62.

59

You pick up the Hand of Glory.

Seriously? You didn't even pause for a second and consider: *Hey, maybe I should put on a glove or something?* Or: *I wonder if this thing has a mind of its own?* No, you just picked it up like it was a stick lying in the gutter. That's—wow—real smart of you.

Now, don't get all fussy about this. Don't whine: "But you told me too!" We're saying—oh, for crying out loud, let's just skip ahead.

Let's see: . . . wooziness . . . black streaks in your vision . . . something's in your blood . . . bla bla bla . . . eldritch intelligences . . . soul devourers . . . don't touch the client . . . and . . . darkness.

So much for your soul. Oops.

EVEN THOUGH THIS HAS BEEN A NON-SCORING EDUCATIONAL ASSESSMENT EXERCISE, WE WOULD LIKE TO POINT OUT THAT YOU DID BADLY.

NO COFFEE VOUCHER FOR YOU.

60

The line reforms around the hand. Occasionally, someone shrieks when they think it twitches, but it doesn't move. It malevolently points in a north by northwest direction.

After a half hour or so, your guard duty is interrupted by a trio. The first guy is broad across the chest, and he clearly cuts his own hair. He's got a heavy leather glove on his right hand, and there's a swagger to him that is both off-putting and attractive. You feel a little dirty having the thought you just had.

He's followed by a woman who looks like your grandma would if she hadn't been ravaged by that necrotic disease she picked up in Central America. She's a librarian on a mission, and you can't help but notice how charming her tortoise-shell eyeglasses are. She even wears them with a thin silver chain. She's adorable, but at the same time, you suspect she would shank you in a heartbeat if it meant saving the world. You idolize her for a moment.

The last member of the trio looks worse than you did after that two-day bender last week. Oh, we know you're trying to forget it, but you did some serious damage to your liver and kidneys. And some dog did pee on you while you were sleeping in the alley. You were a mess.

However, this person looks worse. Like four dogs and an elephant peed on them while they were rolling in garbage. A noxious French cigarette hangs out of the corner of their mouth, and the haze of smoke follows them like an eager sycophant.

"Stand clear. Stand clear," the librarian says.

The big dude leans on the counter and winks at one of the baristas, who immediately blushes.

The walking disaster approaches you and the Hand of Glory. They barely glance at you. "I put on pants for this?" they mutter, and for a second, you think they are talking about you.

"It's—I'm—people could have been hurt," you stammer.

Smoke curls around their head as they look at you. Their eyes are so bloodshot they appear red. "People get hurt all the time," they say, and your heart seizes for an instant as you get a momentary glimpse of the burden they carry.

"Did you touch it?" the walking disaster asks.

You shake your head.

"Good for you," they say. When they look at you again, you feel as if they actually looked at you this time. You feel sort of proud, and disgusted. But mostly proud.

"All clear," the librarian says.

The walking disaster sucks on their cigarette, making the tobacco crackle and howl. They see your hunger and they offer the cigarette to you. You're not sure why you take it, but you do.

They smile, and a trickle of smoke seeps out of their left nostril.

You don't remember anything else, except you're pretty sure you saved the world.

THIS HAS BEEN A NON-SCORING EDUCATIONAL ASSESSMENT EXERCISE.

THE NIGHT OFFICE FIELD TEAM YOU ENCOUNTERED IS MERELY A HYPOTHETICAL EXAMPLE OF THE SORTS OF INDIVIDUALS YOU MIGHT MEET. THE NIGHT OFFICE IS AN EQUAL OPPORTUNITY EMPLOYER, ACROSS A WIDE VARIETY OF FAITHS, CULTURES, RACES, CREEDS, SEXUALITIES, GENDER DESIGNATIONS, AND PSYCHOLOGICAL PROFILES.

AS COMPENSATION FOR YOUR TIME, WE'D LIKE TO OFFER YOU A COMPLIMENTARY COFFEE VOUCHER.

Go to 62.

61

The opposite page has been intentionally left blank—no, this time we mean it—so that some people (we're not naming names) can visit a happy place, free of judgement or error. Nothing happens here. Nothing can kill you. Stay as long as you like, but don't stay too long.

Why not? Because being sedentary will kill you too. Life is like that.

When you feel rested and centered:
Go to 8.

If going to 8 seems too arbitrary:
Go to 14.

62

The coffee voucher enclosed here is redeemable at discerning coffee shops which understand how thin the layers are between this reality and the cosmic vastness where inhuman intelligences dream.

These coffee shops may have additional requirements for use of this complimentary voucher. The Night Office is not responsible for, nor does it have any knowledge of, these additional requirements.

The Night Office urges responsible behavior while self-medicating with all manners of chemical stimulants.

PORTIONS OF THIS EDUCATIONAL ASSESSMENT EXERCISE HAVE BEEN UNDERWRITTEN BY ASPHYXIATION INTERNATIONAL, WHOSE MISSION IS TO REDUCE THAT CREEPING SENSE OF DREAD THAT PERSISENTLY TRIES TO BLOCK YOUR AIRWAYS AT NIGHT.

REMEMBER TO BREATHE. THIS FEELING WILL PASS.

COFFEE

$3

Complimentary
Coffee Coupon

THREE DOLLARS

This coupon has no commercial value, except at those fine dining establishments which observe the sacro-religious evening celebrations related to the convergence of the twin suns of Carcosa, as noted in the neglected correspondences of Eurth, Horas, and Veerdümanken.

63

As you reach for the leather bag, a machine in the wall goes *bing!* and the panel starts to shut. You snatch the leather bag and yank it out of the hole. Your heart is racing. You feel like you've just snatched a precious artifact out of a terrible trap.

Except . . . what's that smell? Is it coming from the bag? Is it the bag itself?

You check the bag. It's not leaking. That's good. But the smell—*oof,* it's definitely coming from the bag. Maybe this wasn't a good idea, after all.

Shove the bag onto a shelf and get the hell out of there.
Go to 66.

Oh, come on. You had a voucher. It opened the safe. You were supposed to find this bag.
Go to 69.

64

You're no expert on occult artifacts, but you do know that if you need to cut off a man's hand and preserver it, you probably have some nefarious purpose in mind. Maybe some kind of sympathetic magic ritual or something. Or maybe it's used to scare kids at Halloween. Regardless, it's not something you need in your life, right?

You shove the hand back in the bag. There's no way to get the safe open again, and you look around for somewhere to stash the hand. There's a file cabinet against the wall next to the storeroom door. You pull open the bottom drawer, intending to ditch the hand and . . .

There's another cloth bag in the drawer, identical to the one in your hand, though much bigger. Bowling ball sized, in fact. Or maybe there's a . . .

Hell, no. Seriously.
Go to 68.

What is going on at this coffee shop?
Go to 71.

65

You don't touch the bag in the wall safe, and after a few moments, the machine in the wall goes *bing!* again. The panel slides shut, and you breathe a sigh of relief. You feel like you narrowly missed doing something terrible.

CONGRATULATIONS, YOU HAVE REACHED A CONCLUSION IN THIS NON-SCORING EDUCATIONAL ASSESSMENT EXERCISE. YOUR ABILITY TO THINK OUTSIDE THE NOMINAL RESTRAINTS OF HUMAN PERCEPTION IS ADMIRABLE.

THAT'S IT. WE'RE ALL DONE HERE. EVERYTHING IS ALL NICE AND TIDY. YOU USED THAT VOUCHER ALREADY; WE'RE NOT GOING TO OFFER YOU ANOTHER ONE.

66

You look around the storeroom for a good hiding place. Behind that stack of toilet paper rolls looks like as good a place as any. Someone will find the bag eventually. You won't care. You'll be long gone.

CONGRATULATIONS, YOU HAVE COMPLETED THIS NON-SCORING EDUCATIONAL ASSESSMENT EXERCISE.

HOWEVER, SINCE YOU USED THE VOUCHER ALREADY, WE CAN'T OFFER IT TO YOU AGAIN. AND SINCE YOU DITCHED YOUR CONSOLATION PRIZE, WE DON'T HAVE ANYTHING ELSE TO OFFER YOU . . .

67

Where were we? Oh, yes, talking about the hand. Yes, it looks like it was harvested professionally. One cut, straight and precise. You don't know the exact formula for pickling human flesh, but whatever solution was used did a nice job of keeping the flesh intact.

You slide the hand out of the bag. It's a left hand, and there are some tattoos on the backs of the fingers, after the second knuckle. The pickling process hasn't helped, but you think each symbol is a letter, although you don't recognize the alphabet. Dried wax is crusted on the back of the hand and between several of the fingers.

What could this be used for?

Maybe the wax is a clue?
Go to 70.

Perhaps there's an instruction manual in the bag?
Go to 73.

68

You drop the bag with the hand in the bottom drawer. The drawer doesn't want to close all the way, and you have to shove things a bit to get it to latch. There. Out of sight. Out of mind.

Time to get the hell out of this place before you find the rest of the body.

CONGRATULATIONS, YOU HAVE COMPLETED THIS NON-SCORING EDUCATIONAL ASSESSMENT EXERCISE.

HOWEVER, SINCE YOU USED THE VOUCHER ALREADY, WE CAN'T OFFER IT TO YOU AGAIN. WE HESITATE TO SUGGEST THAT THE MUMMIFIED HAND WAS A CONSOLATION PRIZE, BUT PERHAPS, IT IS BEST TO PRETEND NONE OF THIS EVER HAPPENED.

IF YOU CAN . . .

69

Gagging a little, you undo the silver string around the neck of the bag. The smell is worse when you open the bag (which isn't surprising, really), and you move to the center of the storeroom so you can get a better look at what is inside the bag.

It looks like . . . well, it looks like a mummified hand. The cut at the base of the wrist is nice and precise. The end has been—

Oh, hell no. You are not going to get all curious about this.
Go to 64.

Well, this isn't that much of a surprise, really. You knew there was something weird about this coffee shop.
Go to 67.

70

Why would someone drip candle wax on a mummified hand?

Yes, we're skipping past the part where we ask why someone would want a hand like this in first place. Stick with it.

Wait. Now that you look at the way the wax has dripped on the hand, you realize the pattern suggests that it came from someone having shoved a candle between the fingers of the hand. Yes, that's more like it. That would explain why the blobs of wax are clustered close to the knuckles. You can see it now: a candle, rising out of the hand like a stiff middle finger.

You look around the storeroom. Maybe the coffee shop sells candles as part of some holiday package . . . Oh, look. Here we go. On a top shelf, you find a couple of seasonal gift packages. One is a romance package. It's got wrapped chocolates, a tiny book of poetry, and a pair of pale pink votives. While the packaging claims the candles will "enhance the intimacy of an evening just for two," you suspect that claim might not hold true with the hand in attendance.

Regardless, you tear open the packaging, scattering the chocolates all over the storeroom floor, and grab one of the votives. You force two fingers apart and shove the votive between them.

Now you just need to find a way to make fire.

Hang on. Isn't this getting a little—dare we say?—a little *out of hand*?
Go to 76.

Surely, there are employee lockers or something back here. In this high-pressure restaurant sales environment, someone has to be a smoker.
Go to 78.

71

On the one hand, you know this is only a mental test. It's just an exercise, meant to test your problem-solving and deductive reasoning skills. But, at the same time, you feel like you're about to pass beyond the realm of the imagination and into something . . . else. This is what the old pulp writers were talking about when they wrote stories about having dreams of strange cyclopean cities that were inhabited by monsters that couldn't possibly exist. How do these abominations communicate across time and space with us? Could it happen through something as simple as a page of text?

Oh my god. Is that what is going on? Are you being influenced by an alien mind?
Go to 72.

No one is coercing you. You just want to know what is in the bag.
Go to 75.

72

In fact, coercion by an alien intelligence is one of the persistent dangers faced by Night Office field operatives. There are, after all, somewhere around a hundred alien intelligences that are eager to swarm our world. Our planet is warm and green. We are soft and tasty. Wherever they are is undoubtedly cold and dark. They are always hungry. They are always seeking new life-forms to dominate and devour. It is only because of the Night Office's constant vigilance that this planet hasn't been turned into a meat farm for the voracious appetites of, say, the Courts of Yjjharlm, who have a long history of sending their tentacled gibber-goats to devour entire civilizations.

Imagine a creature the size of a compact car with four mouths and eighteen tentacles. These gibber-goats are tasked with gathering food for their masters. Once they swallow several hundred pounds of fresh and bloody meat, they return to their master where they vomit—

You know what? That's not important right now. Let's not get ahead of ourselves. The important thing is to figure out if a Yjjharlm Psychic Dominator is trying to coax you into doing something stupid, like using this hand to open a gate between here and there.

Shh. Listen. Can you hear teeth chattering? How about the stamping of hooves?

You don't hear anything.
Go to 74.

Hang on. Maybe you do hear something . . .
Go to 79.

73

Inside the leather bag, you find a worn slip of folded parchment. You peer at the faded writing on the slip.

> *This hand once belonged to Peter Gulliver, a Thief. It was removed from his body shortly after his death by hanging in the year 1614. This hand was used by members of the Black Triangle Gang during the Great Fire of London in 1666. Eighteeen people were known to have died as a direct result of the use of this hand.*

Well, there you go. It's a Hand of Glory. Now, a Hand of Glory, when accompanied by a candle held by the dead fingers, will transfix anyone who looks upon it. Thieves use artifacts like this to get in and get out of secure locations.

Oh, what? Why is the hand here? That's an excellent question. Maybe it's a . . . okay, okay. Yes, we were testing you. We're curious what you would do if you got your hands on a magical artifact that would allow you to sneak undetected into any place you wanted?

Yeah, you don't want this responsibility.
Go to 66.

This is a trick, isn't it?
Go to 76.

74

Well, maybe *that* noise was just someone steaming milk out in the other room. It probably wasn't anything. Just ignore it. What were we talking about? Oh, right. Mental coercion by alien intelligences.

Look, all you were supposed to do was stand in line and use your deductive skills to figure out which of the customers was most likely to open a gate to another dimension and let tentacled monstrosities through. You opted for the turkey and cheddar sandwich instead, which led you to the storeroom of the coffee shop where you—

What?

No, no. This is totally part of the test. Sure, it's not what you were expecting, but come on. This is the Night Office. Every field operation is not what anyone expects.

Anyway, don't overthink things. We're just curious if you can follow directions, even when they seem a bit daft . . .

That's right. Move the hand around a bit. No, not like that. More like—yes, there you go. That's it.

What were we saying? Oh, yes. This test—

Oh, dear. Did the lights just go out in here? That's awkward. What do you suppose happened?

If only there was a way to make a light. Maybe there's something in the leather bag that might help . . .

Good idea.
Go to 82.

No, hang on. Why are the lights out?
Go to 84.

75

You're not under any undue influence. You are going to open this other bag because you are curious. You want to know what's in the bag.

Well, get to it, then. The knot is old and it takes you a minute to tug it free. You unwrap the cord from around the bag and—

Oh, wow. This smells worse than the mummified hand. You tug open the bag and look inside . . .

THIS HAS BEEN A NON-SCORING EDUCATIONAL ASSESSMENT EXERCISE. WE APPLAUD YOUR CURIOSITY, AND HOPE YOU APPLY THAT TO EVERY ASPECT OF YOUR PROFESSIONAL AND PERSONAL LIFE.

WE HAD PROMISED YOU A COFFEE VOUCHER, BUT SINCE YOU USED THAT TO GET INTO THE BACK ROOM AT THE COFFEE SHOP, WE DON'T HAVE ANYTHING ELSE TO OFFER YOU.

WELL, EXCEPT A HEAD IN A BAG.

76

This is definitely more than you signed up for, but at the same time, you can't just leave the hand in the storeroom somewhere. You've got to do something with it. You shove the hand back in its leather bag and then drop the bag into a paper sack with the logo of the coffee shop on it. That won't look conspicuous.

Trying to act nonchalant, you leave the storeroom and head for the door of the coffee shop. Everyone who was in line with you has gotten their coffee, and most of them have left. All except for the professional lady in the maroon blouse. She's standing near the door, pretending to be looking at a display of coffee mugs and decorative kitchen products.

Maybe you're just being paranoid, but there's something about her stance that makes you rethink your exit strategy.

Oh, man. She knows what is in the bag. You've got to get rid of it.
Go to 66.

Be cool. Be cool. Just keep walking.
Go to 77.

77

You nod at no one in particular as you walk toward the door of the coffee shop, the paper sack swinging loosely in your hand. As you pass the professional lady, she spins around. There's an enormous pistol in her hand. "Hold it right there," she snaps, aiming the gun at your face.

Wow. It's a really big gun.

You're not really going to steal the hand, are you?
Go to 79.

Run!
Go to 80.

78

Behind a rack filled with six different sizes of cups, you find a row of small lockers. None of them are locked, and you rifle through them quickly. In the third locker you check, you find a pack of cigarettes and a lighter in a worn purse. The lighter takes a few tries, but you manage to get a flame finally.

The wick of the romance votive is coated with wax, and it takes a second to melt, but it does finally light. You wait for something to happen, but nothing does. It's just you, the mummified hand, and the candle shoved into it.

You feel a little silly, and you consider blowing out the candle and hiding the hand somewhere. But the moment passes and you wonder what would happen if you walked out of the storeroom with this hand.

Might as well try it, don't you think?

The candle flickers as you push through the storeroom door, and for a second, you think the flame is going to gutter out.

You look around the coffee shop. The room is still full of people, doing the things one does in coffee shops, but they're all absolutely motionless. You wait a second, during which no one moves. You wait a second more, and still no one moves.

Wow. This is pretty cool.

You walk over to the dirty guy with the hoodie who was a few places back from you in line. He's at the counter right now, caught in the act of digging through a handful of grimy change. He doesn't flinch when you wave your hand in front of his face. You touch him lightly on the arm, and he doesn't move.

In fact, he feels a little cold.

You lean across the counter and touch the barista's hand. She's definitely cold. Her face is frozen, and you can see how her mask of perpetual pleasantry is slipping a little.

You look around the room. Everyone is frozen. Caught between one instant and the next. The light of the candle is reflected in everyone's eyes. It's all they can see.

The old man who was in line when this whole exercise began is still in the store. He sitting in a comfortable chair by the window. His beverage is on the end table next to him. He's gripping the arms of his chair like he's experiencing vertigo.

You crouch down in front of him and hold the hand with the candle closer to his face.

He doesn't look well. In fact, what you thought was a flickering reflection of the candle's flame in his eyes might be something else . . .

Move the candle closer.
Go to 83.

This is getting creepy.
Go to 81.

79

You stand very still as Professional Lady approaches you. "Give me the bag," she says, holding out her hand. You acquiesce to her demand, and as soon as she receives the bag from you, she makes the gun disappear. You're not quite sure how she manages it. It's an awfully big gun, and her blazer is tailored quite nicely.

She bumps your shoulder as she brushes past you. She doesn't even say 'Thank you' as she leaves. For a moment, you wonder who you just gave the mummified hand to. Did you make a terrible mistake?

Well, it was very large gun . . .

THIS HAS BEEN A NON-SCORING EDUCATIONAL ASSESSMENT EXERCISE. TRUST US. YOU DID THE RIGHT THING.

OF COURSE, HOW THAT HAND OF GLORY GOT IN THE COFFEE SHOP IN THE FIRST PLACE IS ANOTHER QUESTION ENTIRELY.

80

You do realize Professional Lady is a Night Office field agent? No? Oh, well, that's unfortunate.

You make it through the door, but that's about it. There's a thunderous noise behind you, along with the sound of breaking glass. Something picks you up and throws you into the parking lot. You bounce off a parked car and flop onto the ground.

You lost the bag somewhere. Oh, there it—

A truck runs over your arm.

That's the last thing you feel.

THIS HAS BEEN A NON-SCORING EDUCATIONAL ASSESS-MENT EXERCISE. INITIALLY, WE WERE INTERESTED IN YOUR OUTSIDE OF THE BOX THINKING, BUT THE RESULTS OF YOUR EFFORTS WERE . . . RATHER MESSY.

PLEASE RECONSIDER YOUR INTEREST IN THE NIGHT OFFICE. YOU MIGHT NOT HAVE THE TEMPERAMENT WE ARE LOOKING FOR.

81

This is definitely creepy, and you decide enough is enough. You go over to the exit, and just before you leave, you blow out the candle. The lights flicker in the coffee shop, and with a lurch you feel in your heart, everyone starts moving again. Sound returns to the coffee shop, and no one seems to have noticed they were suspended in time.

You tuck the hand and candle under your arm and get the hell out of the shop.

CONGRATULATIONS. YOU'VE MANAGED TO STEAL A HAND OF GLORY. A RATHER UNEXPECTED END TO A SIMPLE NON-SCORING EDUCATIONAL ASSESSMENT EXERCISE.

YOU'RE ONLY GOING TO USE THAT FOR GOOD, RIGHT?

RIGHT?

82

You fumble around in the bag, hoping to find something useful. Your fingers encounter two objects, and you pull the first one out. It's long and slender and feels waxy. You hold it up to your nose. It smells of vanilla. You realize it is a thin candle—one of those sorts of tapers that you find on posh dinner settings.

You grab for the other object, and it turns out to be a small Zippo lighter. You snap open the top and rake your thumb across the wheel. A spark flies. You catch a glimpse of the shelves in the store room. Maybe a face. Then you thumb the wheel again. This time, the spark catches and a weak flame blossoms from the lighter.

Your breath catches in your throat as your brain finally processes what you saw in the spark a moment before. You turn slowly, holding out the flickering flame of the lighter.

The creature lurking in the storeroom with you hisses angrily. Tentacles around its toothed maw wave menacingly.

The hand, you think. When I waved the hand around, I opened something I shouldn't have.

The monster leaps. You drop the lighter. Tentacles and teeth grab you . . .

EVEN IN NON-SCORING EDUCATIONAL ASSESSMENT EXERCISES, THERE ARE HORRIBLE WAYS TO DIE. THIS IS ONE OF THEM. THE GIBBER-GOATS OF YJJHARLM ARE RATHER VICIOUS WHEN THEY TEAR THEIR PREY INTO BITE-SIZED PIECES.

83

You move the candle closer to the old man's face. The movement in his eyes grows more frantic. It's not the candle flame. It's something else entirely.

As you are gawping at the old man, his left eye pops. A long black hook pushes out. His expression doesn't change. He can't feel what is happening.

You stumble back, nearly dropping the hand in your panic.

More barbed hooks push out of the old man's ruined eye socket. His right eye ruptures too, and the bridge of his nose starts to splinter. As you watch in horror, the front of the old man's face disintegrates as a cluster of hook-ended appendages force their way into this world.

The old man's head starts to swell, and you know what is going to happen next.

Oh, it's time to go. Definitely time to go.
Go to 85.

It's the candle. You've got to put out the candle!
Go to 86.

84

Why did the lights go out? Is it a coincidence? It can't be. Something happened when you waved the hand. Did you invoke a summoning spell or something? What the hell were you thinking?

You try to figure out where the door is, and as you shuffle around, you stumble over something that hisses.

Well, that's not good . . .

EVEN IN NON-SCORING EDUCATIONAL ASSESSMENT EXERCISES, THERE ARE HORRIBLE WAYS TO DIE. THIS IS ONE OF THEM. IT'S PROBABLY FOR THE BEST THAT YOU CAN'T SEE THE GIBBER-GOAT OF YJJHARLM. IT WOULD ONLY MAKE THE LAST FEW SECONDS OF YOUR LIFE THAT MUCH MORE TERRIBLE . . .

85

You drop the hand and bolt for the exit. Behind you, the old man's head ruptures. As you reach the door, you glance over your shoulder. The thing that is climbing out of the ruined skin of the old man is something out of an arachnaphobe's nightmare. It has long legs, with barbed hooks at the end; it has dozens of eyes, most of which are staring at you; and its mouth is filled with hooked mandibles.

You yank on the door, and you almost get out.

Something grabs your ankle and you fall down. You scrabble at the door, trying to grab on to it, but you are yanked back into the coffee shop before you can get a good grip.

You roll over as you are dragged across the floor. White silk is wrapped around your legs, and the other end is connected to the spider godling that has crawled into this dimension. It is reeling you in, readying to encase you in lots and lots of silk.

A young woman in a summer dress sitting in a comfortable chair nearby twitches. The top of her head bubbles and tears. Another spider creature forces its way out of the frozen body.

Oh, dear. These two monsters are going to fight over your body . . .

EVEN IN NON-SCORING EDUCATIONAL ASSESSMENT EXERCISES, THERE ARE HORRIBLE WAYS TO DIE. THIS IS ONE OF THEM. THE DARK SPIDER GODLINGS, THE CULTS OF WHICH WERE WIPED OUT THOUSANDS OF YEARS AGO, ARE ALWAYS HUNGRY . . .

86

You lick your fingers and quickly pinch out the flame of the candle. The flame hisses and goes out, and the world lurches around you. One second, everyone is frozen; the next second is a riot of motion as everyone comes back to life. People start babbling, trying to understand what just happened.

The old man slumps over in his chair. Blood leaks out of his ruined eye. His other eye stares at you. There is a look of horror on his face. For a moment, as the enchantment of the Hand of Glory winked out, he was aware of the spider godling that was forcing its way into this dimension through him. The shock has killed him, and you feel bad that he died in terror.

But . . . everyone else is alive.

We call that a 'win' in the Night Office.

CONGRATULATIONS. YOU HAVE SUCCESSFULLY NAVIGATED THIS NON-SCORING EDUCATIONAL ASSESSMENT EXERCISE. WE APOLOGIZE FOR THE LACK OF COFFEE VOUCHER, BUT WE FEEL ITS USE WITHIN THE NARRATIVE LED TO A MORE FULFILLING EXPERIENCE.

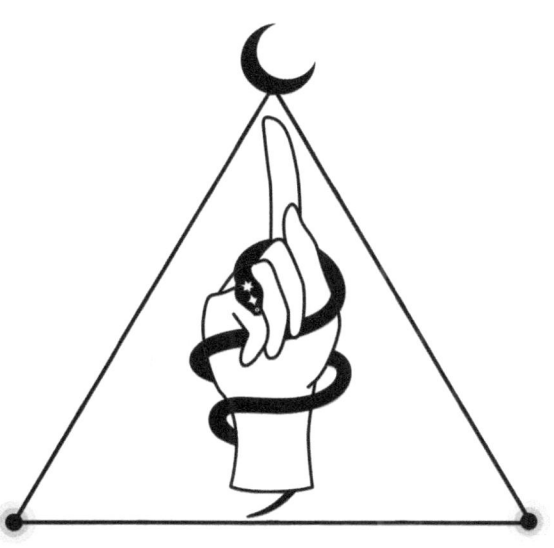

CERTIFICATION: Additional certification opportunities are available from the Night Office
website. Please visit at your earliest conve-
nience and explore those opportunities.

Sign up for the newsletter to be informed
of future educational exercises and training
manuals, as well as other occupational possi-
bilities.

www.nightoffice.org